D1006216

Sparrow's Treasure

by
Anne Schraff

The Perfection Form Company
Logan, Iowa 51546

Cover: Doug Knutson

1 "THAT'S WHELAN!" THE girls behind Rachel Dorr whispered. Rachel turned to look. Mr. Whelan was an ominous-looking man with long dark hair and metallic-black eyes. He moved quickly. He reminded Rachel of a soldier marching in a parade, straight and proud. He was the new world history teacher at Whitman.

"I have him next period," Rachel said to nobody in particular. She figured there was an outside chance somebody would answer. She often mumbled timid little words half out loud. Then, if nobody answered, she wouldn't be hurt.

The other girls continued talking, ignoring Rachel. "They didn't hear me again," she told herself. "I have such a soft voice." But again, Rachel thought, maybe they didn't *want* to hear her. It was better not knowing that for sure.

Rachel Dorr was sixteen years old. She had lived all her life in this small town and, to be perfectly honest, she didn't have a lot of friends. Or maybe *any* really good friends. She had never belonged to one of those tight little groups of kids who share secrets and giggle together in that knowing sort of way.

"Poor dull sparrow," her Uncle Bruce had called her once. "Hopping here and there like a tiny speck in the big wide world. And nobody paying a bit of attention to you."

Uncle Bruce hadn't meant to be cruel. He was feeling sorry for Rachel. But his words had hurt her deeply. She was about twelve at the time, and she had just begun to notice she wasn't "blossoming" like most girls her age. Uncle Bruce's remark frightened her.

Rachel climbed the stairs to her history class. She usually looked down when she walked. She'd memorized just about every tiny flaw in the stairs' tread. She'd even memorized where kids had stuck wads of gum. She was probably the only kid at Whitman who could tell you there was green gum on the fourth stair from the top.

The history rooms had globes and maps that pulled down. Room 202 had a window from which you could see the basketball court. When class got too boring, you could watch kids practicing. Rachel watched the basketball court a lot. Her grades were never good. To her, school meant just putting in your time.

Rachel sat down in the back of the room. She knew the names of everyone in class, but none of them had ever been to her house, or she to theirs. She had fantasies about being as popular as Lorraine or Phyllis. They were so popular they had to juggle party invitations. Rachel imagined herself turning down wonderful parties because she was going to even better ones.

Larry Craig, who had lived three doors from Rachel all her life, walked through the door. He walked straight to the desk next to Rachel and sat down. "Hi," Rachel said.

"Hi," Larry answered before burying his head in a sports magazine.

Last year Larry had been the hero of Whitman's basketball team. His talent had taken the team to the playoffs. It had been thrilling, even though they had lost the championship game.

Rachel had a long-standing crush on Larry. She had almost tried out for cheerleader last year just to cheer for him. She had thought if she were wearing one of those cute blue-and-gold uniforms and waving pom-poms, she'd catch his eye.

She had even rehearsed some cheers at home when she was alone. She'd jumped up and down in the den yelling, "Gimme a W, gimme an H, gimme an I, T, M, A, N. Whitman! Whitman!" And then Rachel had realized how stupid it was to try out. Who'd vote for Rachel Dorr for cheerleader?

"Have you seen Mr. Whelan?" Rachel asked Larry. She was trying to "stir up a conversation." She'd read that phrase in a novel once. The character had "stirred the cold coals of conversation but the words wouldn't rise from the smokeless ashes."

"No," Larry said.

"I have," Rachel said. "He looks nice." It was a bland, dumb comment and not even true. Mr. Whelan didn't look nice at all. But she couldn't think of anything better to say.

Rachel was the only one in her family who lacked the gift of gab. Her mother was a language teacher and her dad anchored a local T.V. news show. Her sister was majoring in journalism. And her big brother was already a super salesman. Rachel could tell it amazed her parents that she was always tongue-tied.

"I hear Whelan is a creep," Larry finally said.

The door opened and in strode Mr. Whelan, carrying a battered, liver-colored suitcase. He stopped for a minute and looked at the class. A look of near hatred rolled across Mr. Whelan's face. He couldn't have looked more disgusted if there had been a huge, horror-movie cockroach perched at each desk wiggling its antenna at him. Rachel wondered if anybody else noticed.

Mr. Whelan sighed. His shoulders sagged like he'd just heard some really bad news. He scrawled his name on the board, then fumbled around for the textbook. He opened the book and thumbed through it as though he were seeing it for the very first time.

Marcia Kenerly raised her hand immediately. "When are we having our first test?" she asked in her sugar-sweet voice.

Mr. Whelan's gaze spun, then settled on Marcia like an angry, buzzing green fly. "What? *What* did you say?" he hissed.

"Our f-first test," Marcia sputtered. Rachel figured Marcia knew by now she shouldn't have asked the question.

Mr. Whelan shot his hand out as if he were trying to hit somebody in the front row. Several of the kids flinched. But then he drew back his hand and looked at his watch.

"Class has been underway exactly two minutes, and you are asking about the first test!" he screeched. "Perhaps you'd like to know about the final exams as well! I cannot fathom this!"

"What's a fathom?" Hank Dunbar

asked. Hank wasn't very smart. But he was a good basketball player, so he had many friends.

Mr. Whelan's lips clearly formed the words "Shut up!" but he stopped himself in time. Instead he yelled, "Silence!" To Rachel, that sounded a lot more impressive.

Rachel was fascinated by Mr. Whelan. She couldn't recall the last time a stranger had ever come to teach at Whitman. It seemed all the other teachers had been friends and neighbors.

For instance, Rachel's mother had gone to school with Rachel's English teacher, Ms. Loring. And Larry's father and the biology teacher were fraternity brothers in college.

It was supposed to be like a big, happy family. And it was—some of the time . . .

"Creep," Larry muttered under his breath.

Rachel didn't think Mr. Whelan was a creep, but she knew the name would probably stick. In this small town where everybody knew everybody else, you were labeled when you were a little kid and that label stuck forever. From first grade on, kids were pegged as bright and popular or dull and uninteresting.

Ms. Loring told Rachel's mother once, "Well, two of yours have been so outstanding. It's almost time for a little disappointment. Oh! I still remember your Denise in my English class! What a delight to teach that girl. But listen, Rachel isn't a poor student . . . she's just average. And she's not a bit of trouble. Why, half the time you don't even know she's there!"

And so everyone knew the best thing to be said for Rachel Dorr was that you didn't even know she was there. She just drifted from room to room like a shadow.

The teachers knew, the librarian knew, and even wrinkled Mrs. Keefe who lived in the corner house knew Rachel was a cobweb-gray person. But Mr. Whelan didn't know! He disliked *all* the students, and that made Rachel feel better. Of course, he'd find out soon enough. The teachers' grapevine would set him straight. But he didn't know yet.

Mr. Whelan began to lecture about cave people. There was a fine madness about him. He prowled from one side of the room to the other, jerking down the maps as if he were angry at them.

Rachel couldn't take her eyes off him for fear she'd miss him doing something awful, like ripping a map clear off the wall. He spun the globe fiercely and jabbed at countries as if he were at war with them. He reminded Rachel of an angry spirit pacing the faded tiles of the classroom.

As Mr. Whelan lectured, the kids wrote frantically. He had said that *everything* would be on the test. Nobody had ever met a teacher like him. When the bell finally rang, the students flooded from the room like a river escaping a dam.

All of the kids were anxious to share their hatred of Mr. Whelan. Little groups of friends came together to talk.

"Did you ever see anything like this guy?" Larry demanded at the soft drink machine.

"He's nuts if you ask me," Hank fumed.

"Really rude," Marcia whispered as she nibbled on a nectarine. Nobody had ever been rude to Marcia before. Her mother always crooned, "The whole world loves my Marcy! She's just so lovable!"

But Mr. Whelan didn't like Marcia, and that warmed Rachel's insides. Maybe it was hateful for her to feel that way, but she admired Mr. Whelan for not liking Marcia.

"He won't last," Ellie Sherman pronounced in her high and mighty voice, tossing her short curls. She was in a position to know. Her father, Harry Sherman, was principal.

Rachel said nothing, as usual. But for the rest of the day she thought constantly about Mr. Whelan. In all her other classes, her kind and knowing teachers didn't expect much from her. "That's good *for you*," Ms. Loring would say in her syrupy voice as she accepted one more of Rachel's sloppy essays. "An acceptable translation, Rachel," Mr.

French (who taught Spanish) would assure Rachel, though she'd faked it.

But Mr. Whelan scowled furiously at everybody, including Rachel, demanding effort. So Rachel took three pages of notes without even realizing it. Three pages of notes instead of her usual doodling!

When school was over, Rachel watched Mr. Whelan gallop to his camper. She usually went directly to her bike and pedaled home. She was never involved in after school stuff. But now a weird impulse struck. She wanted to see where Mr. Whelan lived. She decided to ride her bike in the direction he had gone.

Mr. Whelan turned off the main highway about a mile from school. Traffic was heavy because there was a white sale at Germaines, right on the main street. Crowds of shoppers were coming in and out. That slowed Mr. Whelan down, so Rachel had little trouble keeping him in sight. But then he turned off onto a dirt road going south.

Rachel hesitated, but not for long.

She'd come this far. What harm was there in going a bit farther?

He headed for some dry, grassy hills that were tender green for a few days in spring and dry, haystack yellow for the rest of the year. Rachel saw no houses in the direction he was going. Then suddenly, near a row of eucalyptus trees, he stopped. Rachel kept pedaling until she'd almost reached him. She knew this was stupid, but she just didn't seem able to stop herself.

Mr. Whelan climbed from the camper, pulled off his coat, rolled up his shirt sleeves, and yanked a shovel from the back of the camper shell. He began to climb a small hill. Then, abruptly, he turned and saw Rachel. He stood, just staring at her, like a statue. Rachel immediately broke out in a cold sweat. She felt like a total idiot.

Rachel's first thought was to run. She was going to turn her bike around and pedal home like crazy. But she'd have to face Mr. Whelan tomorrow at school and explain this ridiculous behavior. So she decided not to do that. She wanted to say something, but her mouth was as dry as late-summer tumbleweeds.

Mr. Whelan walked a little down the hill toward Rachel. "Rachel-something, isn't it?"

His hair was disheveled from the strong afternoon wind, and his eyes looked even wilder than they had looked in the classroom.

Rachel suddenly thought he might be a true madman. She was terrified. She knew she'd made a big mistake in following him. Of all the dumb things she had ever done, this was the dumbest!

"You seem to have a penchant for doing the wrong thing, dear," her father often chided. And now, looking down at the tops of her sneakers, Rachel said in a faint voice, "Rachel Dorr."

"Well?" Mr. Whelan demanded.

"Well, what?" Rachel stammered.

His eyes snapped and flashed at her. He seemed barely in control of himself. "What do you want?" he asked, caught between rage and disbelief. Rachel figured he'd never met anybody as stupid as she was.

"Uh ... nothing ... I was just riding my bike and ... I ... well ... I wondered, you know, where you were going."

"You followed me?" he gasped. Rachel could just imagine what he was thinking: These dull, wretched students he hated so much—do they even follow a person home from school? Is there no escape from them?

"I was just ... ah ... curious where you lived," Rachel said, trembling now. She almost bit her tongue as she spoke. She hoped the man wouldn't aim his shovel her way.

"I'm digging a cave for myself to live in right here," Mr. Whelan said.

2 RACHEL ALMOST SAID, "Oh, that'll be nice." When she was nervous, she always believed foolish things people told her, and she always said foolish things back. That made her seem more stupid than she was.

But before she could get her foot in her mouth, Jeremiah Whelan smiled. He looked astonishingly handsome when he smiled. She got numb all over, and big goose bumps popped out on her arms.

"Actually, I'm looking for artifacts," Mr. Whelan said. "Do you know what they are?"

Rachel nodded so furiously she made herself dizzy. "Like archeologists dig up—to see how people used to live ages ago."

Deep in Rachel's heart she blessed that dull television program she'd watched one Sunday night. It had been all about the Olduvai Gorge in Africa, and that's how she knew what artifacts were.

"Right," Mr. Whelan said, continuing to smile. "You know, in that classroom today, I'd mentally singled you out as a bright girl. 'That one can learn something,' I said to myself."

Rachel's mouth dropped open, and she had to remind herself to shut it. She couldn't believe such a clever man could be making such a mistake. But it sounded good, so good. She clung to his words like a drowning person clings to a capsized boat. It might sink soon, but—for a few minutes—you're okay.

"I'm looking for things from the Llano culture, dating back twenty thousand years ago. Particularly, I'm looking for what we call clovis-type points. They used them to bring down large animals," he said.

Rachel was touched that he was sharing so much with her, though she didn't understand a lot of it. Nobody had ever talked to her about important things before.

"Sounds interesting," Rachel said. She was grateful that she'd been able to pull a decent comment from her confused brain.

"It is. Of course, most students your

age wouldn't think so. I sometimes fear you kids watch too much television. And it's turned your brains into tapioca pudding."

"I don't watch much television," Rachel said eagerly. The truth was, she didn't. She preferred reading poetry to watching television. Nineteenth-century poetry, that is—because it was romantic and pretty. Modern poetry was a different story; she didn't know what it meant.

But she loved old poetry and writing in her secret journal. Her writing was only scrambled notes, but she was sure she'd die of shame if anybody got hold of it.

"I'm not surprised that television doesn't interest you," Mr. Whelan said. "You strike me as someone who has little use for that trash."

He came a step closer and asked, "Are you interested in archeology at all?"

"Oh yes," Rachel said, entirely to please him. If he'd asked her if she was interested in learning to play the xylophone with her teeth, she'd have said yes just to stay in his good graces.

"I don't suppose you'd like to work with me on this project? A girl like you probably has a dozen other activities—sports, clubs, dates ... " Mr. Whelan smiled and winked, as if he were talking to a pretty, popular girl, not plain old Rachel Dorr. It was as though he were blind to Rachel's wispy, dull, brown hair and her funny little face that hadn't changed since she was eleven years old.

"Oh, I'd love to work on this," Rachel said quickly.

Mr. Whelan seemed pleased. "Wonderful. After school, you could help me for an hour or so here at the site. I'll pay you an assistant's wages."

"Oh, you wouldn't have to pay me!"

He laughed. "An assistant is worthy of her hire. See you tomorrow then, eh?"

"Oh yes! Thank you, Mr. Whelan."

"One more thing before you go, Rachel. Tell your parents what you'll be doing for me, but don't talk about it at school. I don't want this site crawling with clods from school—especially some of those yokels I met today."

Rachel couldn't imagine a sophisticated teacher like Mr. Whelan confiding in her about her fellow students! It set her apart and made her feel important. All her life she'd felt lower than everybody else. And now all of a sudden, she was above them!

Rachel pedaled home, her mind buzzing with thoughts. She was going to help Mr. Whelan look for Indian artifacts! For clovis points! An assistant he'd said. An assistant!

He'd noticed her. He'd picked her out from among the others as a Somebody. He'd somehow overlooked lovely Marcia and bright Lorraine, pretty Patricia and clever Phyllis. He'd overlooked all the others. He picked Rachel! She hugged that thought to her chest like a warm teddy bear.

Rachel rarely stopped at the library. It sat at the corner of Broad and Maine, a chunky gray building that reminded her of a block of ice. But today, she stopped there before going home.

Rachel marched right up to the desk and asked, "Mrs. Alsted, do you have any good books on Indian artifacts?"

Mrs. Alsted adjusted her glasses and looked at Rachel. She smiled a little. Rachel thought it was weird how some people can put you down with just a tiny turn of their lips.

Before becoming town librarian, Mrs. Alsted had taught third grade. It was in her class that one of the most awful experiences of Rachel's school life occurred: Rachel had accidentally overturned the fishbowl. She still remembered everyone diving for all those slippery goldfish on the floor.

Now Mrs. Alsted gave Rachel that sly smile again and said, "Well, Rachel, are you managing to stay away from fishbowls these days?" She followed this gibe with a chipper little laugh. Rachel thought, "Give me a break! That happened eight years ago!"

"Yes," Mrs. Alsted said, coming back from the stacks. "Here we are." She had a fat old book by a real archeologist and a child's book called *Let's Find Out About Indian Cultures*. The child's book was full of pictures and large lettering. She thrust the picture book at Rachel and said, "I'm sure you'll enjoy this simplified book, Rachel. I also found another, but it's much too difficult for you."

Rachel grinned at Mrs. Alsted. "Give me the big book, please."

Mrs. Alsted sniffed and rolled her eyes heavenward, but she signed out the big book to Rachel.

Rachel stuck the book in her bike basket and pedaled the rest of the way home. She thought about the last glimpse she'd had of Mr. Whelan as she left the site. He had taken off his shirt and was working in a frenzy, perspiration streaming down his back.

When Rachel got home, she told her mother about Mr. Whelan.

"He asked you to be his *what*?" she asked, her eyebrows jumping like they did when she heard a funny story.

"His archeology assistant," Rachel said, her voice quivering with pride. "He said he noticed me right away in class, and he thought I'd be good at it." Rachel couldn't remember anytime recently, or maybe ever, that she had had such exciting news to bring home.

Rachel's mother laughed merrily. "You're joking." She continued to stare at Rachel. Suddenly her look turned worried.

"You're not joking. You never joke. But what on earth could the man be thinking? You have no experience with archeology!"

Rachel could tell her mother was turning all sorts of possibilities over in her mind, all of them bad. She frowned and said, "I was talking to Carla Loring the other day. She told me the new history teacher was strange . . . eccentric. I'm not sure I like this at all. I think it bears looking into."

"He's the most wonderful person I ever met!" Rachel almost screamed at her mother.

"Oh, there you go again, Rachel. What have I told you about exaggerating? The most wonderful person indeed! More wonderful than your father I suppose?"

"No," Rachel said, but not because she really felt that way. In her heart she whispered, "Yes, more wonderful than my father because Dad is always disappointed in me, and Mr. Whelan thinks I'm great. Because, even though I know Dad loves me, he's always giving me that look like, 'She's not too swift.'"

"And more wonderful than your brother?" Rachel's mother continued.

"No," Rachel said aloud. Then, to herself, "Yes, because Thomas thinks I'm stupid, too."

"Well then, let's watch our exaggerating, shall we? No more hyperbole. Let's just make sure this Mr. Whelan isn't some dangerous type. I'm not letting you get involved in something without checking it out."

Panic seized Rachel. Her mother was going to ruin it for her—ruin the best thing that had ever happened to her.

"Oh, Mom, please! I gotta do it. I promised Mr. Whelan. Mom, I'll die. I mean I'll absolutely die if I can't do it!"

"Hyperbole again. And not a minute after we discussed it. I think I'll just call Harry Sherman and do a little investigating."

"Mom! Don't mess it up for me!" Rachel pleaded.

"Calm down. Stop jumping around like a twittering sparrow. Honestly, Rachel, sometimes I think your uncle was right. You can be such a silly little thing sometimes. Just like a sparrow on a window sill, hopping hither, thither, and yon. All I'm going to do is ask Harry about Mr. Whelan's background. I'm a parent. I have the right to know."

Rachel sat down in miserable silence as her mother dialed the Sherman house. She just knew her precious chance to be special would be destroyed. She'd have to tell Mr. Whelan she couldn't be his assistant after all!

Then Rachel suddenly realized that her mother was wearing a pleased expression. It was clear that Mr. Whelan was being praised.

"My," Rachel's mother said, "is that right? Then we made quite a catch for Whitman High, didn't we? Yale? He knew Samuel Eliot Morrison? Well, well. That's wonderful."

She put the phone down and looked at Rachel. "Mr. Whelan seems to have a fine background. Are you sure you understood him right? He really wants you as an assistant?"

"Yes," Rachel said beaming.

Later, when Rachel's father came home and listened to the story, he said, "That's the most amazing thing I've ever heard."

No objections! Rachel was delighted everything had turned out okay after all.

Rachel studied her book on Indian artifacts that night. She wanted to know enough so that Mr. Whelan wouldn't be shocked by her ignorance tomorrow. It would spoil everything if he asked her a simple question and she said something stupid.

And then, as Rachel studied, a new worry came to her. Mr. Whelan would find out from the other teachers that he'd made a terrible mistake choosing Rachel Dorr as his assistant. Rachel could just imagine what they'd tell him tomorrow morning in the faculty room.

"Rachel Dorr? You chose *her*? Whelan, old fellow, she's got nothing between the ears. Hahaha."

"Not too bright, that one, a dim bulb."

"Poor thing won't go far on her brains. It's a pity she's not better looking."

Rachel burned with shame just thinking about it. Mr. Whelan would feel like a fool for choosing her.

Rachel leaped from bed and grabbed her English book. Trembling with sudden determination, she decided she'd prove to Ms. Loring that she knew quite a bit, after all. If she could only get to Ms. Loring before she poisoned Mr. Whelan's opinion.

Rachel flipped through the book and found the dreary story she was supposed to read for English tomorrow.

The story wasn't beautiful like Percy Bysshe Shelley's "Ode to the West Wind," or thrilling like Wordsworth's

"Westminster Bridge Sonnet," but Rachel was determined to read and understand it. Tomorrow when they discussed it, Rachel would make a good showing. Perhaps she could change Ms. Loring's awful opinion of her—at least a little bit.

Then Rachel dug out her biology book from under the bed where it had formed a convenient home for spiders. Mr. Fenwick had said something about sketching the different kinds of animal and plant cells. Usually, Rachel ignored homework. But now she did her best to draw the tracheids and paramecium, and the nerve cells that looked like trees.

She was working furiously when her sister, Denise, poked her head in the bedroom door. "What're you doing?"

"My homework," Rachel said, wanting her sister to go away.

Denise laughed. "Since when do you do homework?"

"Since an hour ago. You are looking at a new Rachel Dorr."

Denise laughed again. "Are you nuts

or what?''

"No. Maybe I'm just sick of being the dumb one in the family.''

Denise flopped down on Rachel's desk chair. She'd been dating a boy named Mark, and today they'd gone bowling after her morning classes at college. "You know," she said, "sometimes I think Mark is insensitive.''

Rachel was trying to finish her biology sketches.

"Today, I bowled better than he did, and he was irritated.''

"Guys like to win, I guess," Rachel said. "Look, I gotta finish this for tomorrow. And then I gotta read a dumb story for English.''

"Uh huh," Denise said, getting more comfortable in the chair. "I think I'll go out with Jeff this weekend. Let Mark know I don't like him acting like a jerk.''

"Yeah," Rachel muttered.

"Jeff is really cute.''

"Denise, I gotta concentrate, you know?''

"Concentrate on what?''

"This story for Ms. Loring's class."

"Oh Rachel, she won't flunk you. There were plenty of kids like you in her class when I went to high school. She never flunked them."

Rachel looked at Denise. "I'm sick of being a kid like me," she said, her voice trembling a little.

3 "RAE DORR, WHAT'S wrong with you?" Denise stared at her sister.

"Dinner's ready, girls," Rachel's mother called from the kitchen. When they didn't come immediately, she followed the voices to Rachel's bedroom.

"Mom," Denise said, "Rae is acting weird."

Rachel's mother laughed. "Don't mind her, Denise. This brilliant nut, Mr. Whelan, has decided to let your little sister help him dig up Indian artifacts. She's gone absolutely wild about it."

Denise joined her mother's laughter—laughter at Rachel's expense. Usually when her family treated her this way, Rachel wanted to scream and break something. But this time, she ignored them. She was too happy and excited to let them spoil it.

Rachel biked to school early the next morning. She wore her jeans and a pretty yellow sweater over a faded work shirt. She figured she could pull off the sweater at the dig and work in the crummy shirt.

In English class, Ms. Loring began, "Today, we'll be discussing 'A Strange Afternoon.' It's a complex story about emotions. Who'd like to start by describing the lead character, Mrs. Deems?"

Rachel hardly ever raised her hand to answer a question. Last time was a year ago in history, and then she got Andrew Jackson mixed up with Andrew Johnson and the whole class laughed. But now she forced her arm up.

"Do you wish to be excused, Rachel?"

Rachel gulped hard but stammered, "No, I want to talk about Mrs. Deems."

Everybody laughed, just like they did when Rachel got the two Andrews mixed up. Rachel's face got hot and prickly. Ms. Loring glared at her like she was deliberately disrupting class. Rachel didn't care, though. She just had to prove she'd read the dumb story and, for once, understood it. Rachel kept Mr. Whelan's face in her mind for encouragement.

"Mrs. Deems was this widow, and all she had was a cat, see," Rachel began.

When Rachel had first begun to read

the story, she'd hated it. Then she had read it again, and she had begun to see pieces of herself in Mrs. Deems. Mrs. Deems was lonely too, like Rachel. Nobody would talk to her or pay any attention to her. When she got up the nerve to say something, people would laugh behind their hands and whisper that she was senile.

There was a part in the story when Mrs. Deems got so desperate that she'd talk to her cat and tell the cat how lonely she felt. Rachel was shocked. She herself often poured out her heart to the family dog when nobody else acted like she existed. All of a sudden Rachel almost cried reading the story because *she was Mrs. Deems!*

Other hands went up in the room. It was harder for Rachel to break in again. Finally Ms. Loring said, "If Mrs. Deems loved the cat so much, why did she cry when she found it again after it was lost?"

"She cried from relief?" Larry suggested.

"No, I don't think you're on the right track," Ms. Loring said.

Rachel tensed up because she knew the answer. It was so clear; she couldn't believe all those smart kids couldn't get it. Rachel raised her hand.

Ms. Loring seemed puzzled. "Yes, Rachel?"

"The reason she cried—Mrs. Deems, I mean—well, she didn't know how lonely she was, until the cat went away. Then she got all busy looking for the cat. And when she found it, it hit her real hard what an awful, empty life she led. Since she'd found the cat, it'd go on like before—just her and the cat. Nobody else cared or would ever care."

"That is . . . exactly right," Ms. Loring said in astonishment.

As they walked out of class, Larry said, "Hey, Rachel, how did you know so much about that crazy story?"

"I guess because I felt sorry for the old lady."

"I hated the story."

"I did too, at first, but then I

understood it."

"Why do we have to read stories about old ladies, anyway," Larry grumbled. He was just mad he hadn't gotten it and Rachel had. "They're not like us."

"Yes, they are, Larry. Sometimes, anyway. Mrs. Deems is like me."

"Naw. She was silly to make so much of a cat."

"Not when it was all she had, Larry," Rachel answered. She surprised herself arguing with Larry. Usually she just agreed with what anybody said, especially boys.

Rachel went to biology then and turned in her sketches.

"Excellent!" Mr. Fenwick gasped.

And then finally it was time for history. Rachel kept wondering what it would feel like to be in Mr. Whelan's class today. Considering their special relationship, it ought to feel different. But maybe not. Even though they'd be working together at the dig, he'd probably not make much of it in class.

As she sat down in her seat, she heard

Larry gripe, "Time for the creep show."

"Mr. Whelan isn't a creep," Rachel said.

Larry turned sharply. "Everybody says so."

Ellie Sherman piped up. "I guess he's some big shot. I complained to Dad about him, and Dad said we're lucky to have such a genius teach at our little school. He could be teaching at some big college or something."

"Well, he's still a creep," Larry said.

"He's soooo cute," Marcia said, rolling her eyes in her silly face. "I dreamed about him last night."

Rachel resented Marcia's dreaming about Mr. Whelan. He didn't have a special relationship with *her*. If anybody had the right to dream about Mr. Whelan, it was Rachel, and nobody else.

Rachel smiled inside. If they only knew . . . if they only knew that after school, she and Mr. Whelan would be out at the dig site, side by side in the hills, digging through the dust of the past. They'd be finding something wonderful—maybe a major discovery.

Rachel had read all about the Llano culture last night until her eyeballs ached. But she didn't care. The book had fallen from her hands as she dropped off to sleep at midnight. Now her mind was filled with marvelous phrases like "paleo-Indian stage" and "fluted point stage."

Mr. Whelan bounded in as before, slamming down his battered suitcase and snapping open the textbook. He cast a scowling glance around, then said, "Yesterday we discussed the Neanderthal people. Let's see how little we remember. Glen, in what country do we find the Neanderthal gorge?"

"Uh . . . China?" Glen asked hopefully.

"No! Marcia?"

"The Netherlands?" Marcia ventured, her pink face turning red.

"Good grief!" Mr. Whelan exploded. "Were you all sleeping yesterday? What do you use your minds for around here? The gorge was found in Germany. Germany!" His angry gaze swept the room in search of victims. "Did Neanderthal man learn to cope with the Ice Age . . . Larry?''

"Ah no . . . 'cause that came before,'' Larry mumbled.

"Before what?'' Mr. Whelan demanded.

"Before those Neanderthal guys were on earth, I guess,'' Larry said.

"Well, you *guess* wrong, because Neanderthals took refuge in the caves and used fire to warm themselves.'' He turned again, "How about Neanderthal man's brain size? How did it differ from modern brain sizes?'' He fixed his dark stare on Rachel. "Rachel?''

Rachel froze. Brain size? She remembered everything else about the lecture yesterday, but she wasn't sure about this. "Uh . . . they had very small brains,'' she stammered.

"The same as ours!'' Mr. Whelan shouted so loud the stapler on his desk seemed to jump. He gripped the edge of his desk. "How fortunate the brains in this classroom cannot be tested scientifically! I'm afraid you'd all be profoundly humiliated!''

Rachel felt sick. She wished the faded tiles in the floor would turn liquid and swallow her up forever.

It was all ruined now, of course, her wonderful new status. Rachel could just imagine what would happen at the end of class. Mr. Whelan would call her up to his desk and say, "I'm afraid asking you to be my assistant was a big mistake, Rachel. You seem as stupid as the others. So let's just forget about our arrangement, shall we?" Then she would be dismissed.

Never mind that she'd thought about him constantly since yesterday. Never mind that for once in her crummy life she'd been singled out for a little recognition. Never mind all that. Rachel had blown it all over the size of a cave man's brain!

The last bell rang, and Mr. Whelan's voice came as Rachel knew it must. "Wait, Rachel, I'd like a word with you."

There was no escaping it. Rachel had to go to his desk and listen to the fateful words. She felt like some poor condemned soldier standing at attention while they ripped off her stripes.

Rachel bit back the tears and walked up to the front of the room.

4

MR. WHELAN QUICKLY stuffed
things into his briefcase. He didn't
Look at Rachel as he spoke.
And he didn't see the tears dribbling
down her cheeks.

"If you'll just wait by my camper, I'll
be through here in a few minutes, and
then we can go. Just toss your bike into
the back—the door's open."

Rachel was stunned.

"Sure, yes," she said, her voice
cracking.

In less than five minutes, Rachel and
Mr. Whelan were pulling out of the school
parking lot. As the camper passed the
building, Rachel turned her head and saw
Larry standing by the bike rack. He had
a very shocked look on his face. He
couldn't believe Rachel was riding off
with Mr. Whelan!

Rachel shook her head and then turned
to Mr. Whelan. "I did a lot of reading
about the Llano culture last night," she
said quickly, before she lost the nerve to
speak to him at all. "They hunted
mammoths, didn't they? I didn't think

there were big animals around here."

Rachel thought her voice sounded high pitched and squeaky, like a ten year old's. But it was the best she could do, and she was lucky she could do that.

"Oh sure." He didn't seem to notice how her voice sounded. "It was wetter and cooler around here than it is now. Lush grasses grew then—perfect for the woolly mammoths and the bison."

As they drove, Rachel stared at his profile. He was so beautiful! "Do you . . . uh . . . like teaching at Whitman so far, Mr. Whelan?"

Rachel expected he'd say something phony like most adults, especially teachers. Teachers were expected to like what they're doing, even though many didn't and all the kids knew it. Mr. Fenwick told the parents he loved teaching. Yet half the kids heard him grumbling, saying he'd take a different job in a minute if he could get it.

"If I tell you the truth, Rachel, can you keep it a secret?"

"Yes," she said.

"Well," Mr. Whelan smiled until the smile became a grimace, as if he were in pain, "I hate it. I loathe it. I'm used to dealing with adults, and I had no idea how ghastly it would be to teach high school. It's enough to rot the mind and give one gangrene of the soul."

Rachel almost laughed at his shocking honesty. "Then, why did you come here?" In her excitement over talking to him like a regular person, she forgot to be nervous.

"The dig, Rachel. I'm fascinated by Indian artifacts. During the summer, I stumbled across some promising test holes in the region. I think I'm onto something really exciting, but I need to support myself while I dig. Hence, the teaching job at Whitman."

"I hope I can help you," Rachel said, instantly feeling it was a stupid comment. What could a sixteen year old who didn't know the first thing about archeology do to help?

"I'm sure you can, Rachel. You're just the kind of person I need: a serious, dependable student. You're really very mature for your age."

"Thank you," Rachel said, deeply moved. She didn't get many compliments—or any, really. She figured she didn't do anything well enough to deserve any.

Once she'd tried to learn sewing, but Denise was so much better that Rachel had given up quickly. It was that way with almost everything she did. Thomas and Denise were superior at everything long before Rachel got to it. Lately, it even seemed hopeless to try. She'd only fail in the end.

They pulled onto the site. Rachel saw there was already a deep hole and a mound of dirt beside it. She figured Mr. Whelan had done a lot of digging the night before.

"That's a test hole," he said. "That's how we find out how many layers of artifacts there are in the area. What I'd like for you to do is carefully screen that mound of dirt for artifacts."

He looked at Rachel more closely and continued, "Better take that nice sweater off. Don't want you to ruin it."

Rachel pulled off her sweater and smiled. "I put an old work shirt on under it so I would be ready to dig when I got here."

"Excellent. I admire foresight in a person," he said, kneeling down and taking out the equipment. "Here's the sifting screen and a brush. Just pile a panful of dirt on the screen and sift it like flour. Any artifacts will remain on top. Carefully put them aside and carry the checked dirt over by the shrub. That's our dump site. It's painstaking work. I hope you won't mind it too much."

"Oh, I won't!" Rachel said, excitement making her heart pound. How could he think she'd mind anything she did for him?

As Rachel set to work sifting the dirt, Mr. Whelan began chopping vigorously at the side of the hill with a pick. After a few minutes, he took off his shirt and hung it on a shrub.

Rachel tried not to stare, but it seemed so strange to see a teacher shirtless, sweat streaming, picking at the dirt like a laborer. His muscles rippled under his skin like the waves of the sea. His hands weren't smooth—they were calloused.

Rachel thought of Mr. Payne, who taught chemistry last year. He was young, too, but he was kind of weak and soft. He looked like he'd never lifted anything heavier than a ballpoint pen.

There was something about Mr. Whelan now, a kind of total joy that was missing when he was in the classroom. Rachel knew he'd told her the truth. He really did hate teaching. This is what he loved—looking for something special. And he was letting Rachel share in it!

Rachel went through a lot of dirt without finding anything. Her back ached. And she was disappointed—not for herself, but for him. She wanted to be able to find something good for him, something that'd make him glad he'd chosen her.

Then, as she sifted the tenth panful, the mesh caught something. "Oh!" Rachel gasped out loud.

Mr. Whelan left his pick sticking in the hill and came over.

"What've you got there?"

"I don't know," Rachel said, "but it looks like a spear point."

He reached down and took it. "It's a projectile point all right! See—it's leaf shaped. Oh, this is very encouraging! This is the most promising thing I've uncovered here, yet, Rachel. I knew you'd bring me luck!"

Rachel almost burst with joy. The rest of the hour flew. And though she found nothing else but an old pottery shard, Mr. Whelan had made so much of the projectile point that she didn't care.

"Time for you to go home now," he announced at the end of the hour.

"Oh, I could work longer."

"No. I don't want you riding home on your bike in the dark. Anyway, you have your homework. You've done very well here this afternoon, Rachel. A perfect assistant."

"It was great," Rachel said. "I had fun."

Mr. Whelan lifted Rachel's bike out of the camper while she stood waiting. She didn't mean to look into the camper, but she did. And way in the corner, on the dinette, she saw it. A gun was laying alongside Mr. Whelan's shovels and picks. Rachel sucked in her breath, but he didn't notice.

5 AS SOON AS Rachel pedaled into her driveway, Larry came over. Rachel figured he had been watching for her because he sprinted up right away.

"What were you doing with Whelan?" he bluntly asked. A grim look sat on his face.

In the past, Larry had come over to visit Rachel all the time. But lately, he hadn't been around, and she had missed him. She never really knew why he stopped coming. One day, he just didn't want to be her friend anymore, and Rachel never had any idea why. She had wondered if she'd done something wrong.

But now she resented his coming over and questioning her. He acted like he had a right to know everything about her, but he didn't! Rachel stated simply, "I'm helping with his archeological project."

"What? Are you kidding me?" Larry laughed.

Rachel was furious. For a minute, she hated him. "I really am working with him, Larry."

"Rachel, come on. This is old Larry you're talking to. I know you. What's this guy up to anyway?"

"Larry, Mr. Whelan doesn't think I'm dumb like you do. He respects me. And he doesn't laugh at me. I'm really helping him. He said so."

"Hey, I don't think you're stupid. Where did you get *that* idea? Listen, Rachel, do your folks know you're hanging out with this guy?"

"Yes, they know all about it. Mr. Whelan said to tell them."

"Oh." Larry seemed disappointed. Rachel knew he had been ready to charge into her house and get her in trouble with her parents. "What kind of project did you say it was?"

"Larry, it's none of your business, you know?" Rachel found the courage to go on. "I mean, we used to be friends, but then, all of a sudden, I wasn't even good enough to say hello to at school. And when I try to talk to you at school, you're always busy reading your dumb sports magazines. You act like I'm embarrassing you or something. So just don't bother me now, okay?"

Larry looked hurt. He didn't say anything for a minute. Then he mumbled, "Rachel I . . . ah . . . oh, never mind. See you." He turned and stalked off toward his own yard.

Rachel was trembling a little as she went inside. Nobody was home, so she moved into the living room and plopped down on the couch. She stared up at the family portrait over the mantel. The three Dorr children and their parents smiled happily down at Rachel.

Rachel had never told anybody, but she hated that picture. It was taken when she was six, Denise was nine, and Thomas was fifteen. Even then, you could see the order of quality. Denise and Thomas were very good-looking and Rachel wasn't. Rachel was the ugly duckling. The ugly duckling who would never turn into a swan. Even the photographer who took the picture seemed to push Rachel over to the side as much as possible.

It was the same story in the den. That

was where all of Denise's and Thomas' trophies from sports and school were piled. They were winners and Rachel wasn't.

Rachel would like to have died when she got a crummy blue ribbon in a seventh-grade spelling bee. Her mother made a big thing of hanging it beside her brother and sister's golden prizes. There the limp thing hung, like a badge of shame. It was worse than nothing.

But Mr. Whelan thought Rachel was special. She reminded herself of that fact to drive off the gloom of the portrait and the trophies. Mr. Whelan took the sting out of all her hurts. If a brilliant man like him saw something valuable in her, then something must be there. Maybe she was, after all, a diamond in the rough—the ugly duckling who may never be a swan, but just might become a splendid duck.

Rachel rushed to her room to get started on her homework.

In English the next day, Rachel surprised Ms. Loring again by writing a good essay. And she turned it in on time.

Later, during break, Marcia and Ellie joined Rachel at the whipped chocolate machine.

"Are you really helping Mr. Whelan with a project?" Ellie asked. Apparently, Larry had been talking.

"Yeah," Rachel admitted, trying not to make it sound like a big deal.

"Wow, that's neat," Marcia said. "How did you get in on it? Does he need anybody else?"

"I was a TA for Fenwick last year," Ellie said. "Maybe I could help out, too."

"Mr. Whelan needs just one person. It's very dull work, anyway. Dirty, too." Rachel was glad the bell rang for class. She hurried off while the two girls stared enviously after her.

Rachel basked in their envy. After all, how many times she had envied them! They had their pick of boyfriends. They were cheerleaders and homeroom officers. They were Somebodies all the time, and Rachel was a Nobody.

But now Rachel had something. She was Mr. Whelan's assistant. She was no longer just a shy, quiet kid who faded into the background.

When lunch came, Rachel went to her usual place under the spreading pepper trees. Most of the time she ate alone. But today, Larry came walking up with his brown bag.

"Mind if I sit here too, Rae?" he asked a little sheepishly.

Rachel shook her head. "If you don't mind all the pepper tree berries falling on you." She watched him settle down, relaxing his big, wide shoulders and stretching his long legs. He was handsome all right, Rachel admitted. Especially with that tousled dark hair that matched his eyes so perfectly.

How many times Rachel had gazed at him as he leaped for a crucial basket during a game. How she'd died a thousand deaths when he missed a free throw and some kids booed. How she'd hugged and soothed him in her fantasies, trying to make the hurt look on his face disappear after a painful injury or a defeat. But he'd never seemed to notice.

Not once.

"Boy, what's come over you, Rae?" he asked her suddenly, his eyes on the English textbook open in her lap.

"You mean this?"

"Yeah. You're always studying. And last night when I came over, you seemed so cold . . . like a stranger."

"Well, you sort of *are* a stranger, Larry."

"Me? I've lived a couple of houses from you all our lives. Remember when we'd play checkers summer nights and I'd always beat you?"

"I let you beat me," Rachel said. She'd never admitted that to him before. She'd wanted to please him so badly that when she'd get a chance to jump, she'd pretend she didn't see it. Rachel thought Larry would like her better if she didn't win much and would come over more often. But he stopped coming anyway.

"Why did you let me win?" he asked, genuinely surprised.

"I don't know. So you'd like me, I guess."

"I liked you anyway. I always have."

Rachel concentrated very hard on her sandwich. She had never studied the texture of the bread in such detail. She thought—but didn't say—"If you like me, how come you never took me out? Why did you take out girls like Patty, Phyll, and Marcia?"

Larry finished his sandwich and fumbled with an orange. "I uh . . . was going to ask you to go someplace with me one of these days." It was weird, like he'd read Rachel's thoughts. He cleared his throat and fiddled with an orange peel.

"I wanted to ask you out a lot of times, but you know how some of the guys are. My friends, I mean. They hassle you if you don't date . . . you know, cheerleaders and stuff. But I always wanted to ask you out."

Rachel thought to herself, "Heaven forbid I should make you feel embarrassed in front of your friends." But out loud, she merely said, "You don't have to explain, Larry. Actually, I don't have much time for dates."

"Because of that Whelan guy?" Larry asked, sounding angry. "You want to hang out with him all the time?"

"I don't hang out with him, Larry. We're working on a very important project."

"Yeah, but you could get hurt."

"I don't see how."

"A girl like you and an old guy like him," Larry snapped out the words.

"He's not an old guy. He's the youngest teacher at Whitman. Anyway, what age should teachers be? Should they be sixteen like us? They wouldn't let them teach if they were kids."

"All right, okay. But you know what I mean. You could get a thing about him and he could, you know, take advantage."

"Larry, he loves his work. He's like a fanatic about it. He doesn't even look at me when he's working. You don't know anything about us, about Mr. Whelan and me. We're just both into archeology and we're . . . we're like partners."

Larry said nothing for a minute. He picked up a pepper tree berry and mashed it. "I don't suppose you'd go to the junior picnic with me."

"I'll see if I can make it. I'm not sure," Rachel said.

Larry looked shocked. He stared at her, his mouth slightly open. He couldn't believe Rachel hadn't jumped at the chance for a date with him. He got up quickly, mumbled something about basketball practice, and hurried away.

6 RACHEL FELT TERRIBLE. She'd really wanted to go out with Larry, even though he'd snubbed her for a long time. But now—maybe because of Mr. Whelan—she felt different about herself. She wasn't just somebody to be picked up, discarded, then picked up again. Larry couldn't ignore her for two years, then snap his fingers and expect her to come running. She wasn't a pathetic little nobody—not anymore.

Mr. Whelan was his old crabby self in history. He constantly looked at his watch and seemed to urge the hands of the clock forward with his eyes.

Rachel had never had a teacher who so openly hated what he was doing. Yet, Mr. Whelan was the most energetic teacher she'd ever had. He demanded better work from his students than they had ever done before.

Rachel figured it was because he didn't care how much they hated him. She thought her other teachers demanded so little because they wanted to be popular. Just like the kids.

Not Mr. Whelan. He'd scribble angry criticisms in red ink all over papers and exams. And his spoken comments were even more sarcastic and bitter. He'd say, "Oh, did I wake you up, Marcia?" or "Ignorance is apparently contagious, Glen. Since your inane answer about the tariff, we've had an epidemic of stupidity on our hands."

Even Rachel did not escape his attacks. Yet she forgave him. She certainly didn't want to be teacher's pet. But she was probably the only one who didn't hate Mr. Whelan. In fact, she thought, she loved him in a way.

After class that day, Rachel went straight to the camper and waited for him. He came quickly, hauling his case and grinning happily, glad that another hated school day was over. He ran to the driver's side like a kid on his way to the circus.

How different Mr. Whelan was outside the classroom, Rachel considered. He whistled or hummed almost all the time he drove or worked at the dig.

"What will you do if we find something really terrific at the dig, Mr. Whelan?" Rachel asked as he whistled. "Will you write a book about it?"

"Why, yes. Publish or perish, they say. Then I'll be rich."

"Rich?"

"Of course. Buy a big glass house overlooking the ocean at Monterey. Wear Gucci clothes. Go to Paris in the spring. Ski in Colorado in the winter."

"Do books like that make much money?"

"Books like what?" he asked absently. Rachel figured his mind was still on Paris or something.

"About Indian artifacts and stuff."

"Oh, yes. Well . . . I'm sure some do." Mr. Whelan didn't seem very interested in discussing it. He started whistling again, interrupting himself just once to say, "Cut your hair."

"Excuse me?" Rachel had heard him. She just wasn't sure she'd understood him.

"I saw an old movie on television.

There was a girl in it who reminded me of you. Audrey Hepburn in the movie *Roman Holiday*—you have a pixie face just like hers. You should wear your hair in the same style."

Mr. Whelan braked at the site. But Rachel sat still for a moment, bewildered. She was too stunned to speak. Audrey Hepburn? Rachel wondered what Audrey Hepburn looked like. She couldn't wait for a chance to look her up in one of those movie history books at the library.

Surely this woman couldn't be very attractive if she reminded him of Rachel. But she was an actress, wasn't she? She must have been pretty!

Mr. Whelan was already in motion, dragging out equipment. Picks and shovels and a big chain saw fell together in a heap in the dust. Mr. Whelan quickly grabbed the saw and heaved it back in the van. Rachel watched it disappear as he slammed the door and headed up the hill.

"He must use the chain saw to cut firewood," she reasoned. "We certainly don't need it here. Anyway, there's no gun in sight today, thank goodness."

Still, she glanced uncertainly at Mr. Whelan as he jogged along in front of her. But she saw only the joyful movements of a familiar, kind, and trusted friend. Relieved, she smiled and followed him.

Rachel immediately spotted many new mounds of dirt all around the dig. Mr. Whelan must have worked late into the night after she had left.

Rachel began sifting through mounds of dirt and carrying buckets of it to the dump site. She found a few pieces of broken pottery, but nothing like the day before.

At the end of the hour, she was a little disappointed. But Mr. Whelan said, "Cheer up. You can sift for a week and not find anything. Then suddenly there's the find of a lifetime staring you in the face. That's the fun of it. Like digging for buried treasure.

"That point you turned up yesterday was a gem," he continued. "You're very thorough. I appreciate that.

"Oh, by the way, there's a wretched faculty meeting tomorrow afternoon. By the time the confounded thing ends, it'll be dark! That means we can't work out here tomorrow. But I'll see you on Friday, okay?"

"Oh yes," Rachel assured him.

He went to his camper and took out his wallet. "Ten dollars for two days. Is that about right?"

"Mr. Whelan," Rachel gasped, "that's too much."

He laughed. "Nonsense. And let me give you some advice. Never reject a payment as 'too much,' whatever you get. You're worth it. Most of the time you're worth more than people offer, but you are *never* worth less. Remember that."

He put two crisp five-dollar bills into Rachel's hand and said, "See you Friday."

Rachel looked at him for a minute, wondering if she should say it. Maybe it would sound foolish and he'd laugh. But Rachel had wanted to say it ever since she began working with him.

"Mr. Whelan, you sort of look like Percy Bysshe Shelley. He's my favorite poet."

Mr. Whelan threw back his head and laughed heartily. Then he walked off whistling with the pick over his shoulder.

He hadn't laughed *at* Rachel. He was just pleased by what she had said. She could tell.

On the way home, Rachel stopped at the library. She did not talk to Ms. Alsted this time. Instead, she ran to the reference section where they kept the oversized books.

Rachel thumbed through one until she found what she'd been searching for. There she was: Audrey Hepburn, complete with a fabulous rhinestone necklace and a tiara.

She was gorgeous! Rachel couldn't imagine how her own dull face could remind Mr. Whelan of Audrey Hepburn.

As Rachel pedaled towards home, confused thoughts tumbled in her brain. "The inside of my skull must look like a clothes dryer in high gear," she thought.

Despite all that, Rachel felt great! And she began to see wonderful things all around her that she'd never seen before. Beautiful, bright trees and flowers, for instance. The bird's nest on the scrubby tree at the corner. The yellow roses standing tall and proud in Mrs. Keefe's front yard. Rachel's life suddenly seemed to be blooming along with those yellow roses.

Even school was beginning to be enjoyable. Rachel had to write a short story for English, and she was actually looking forward to it. She decided to use some notes from her journal because they would make the story more real. Her idea was to put her feelings into her character's head and make the story from that. It was the most exciting thing she had ever thought of doing in a class project.

Thomas' car was in the driveway as Rachel pedaled up. Her brother had an apartment in a city about two hundred miles away. But he often came home for long weekends to spend time with the family.

"Hi, funny face." Thomas swung open the front door at the exact moment Rachel came to it. He grabbed and hugged his sister.

"Hi, Tom," Rachel said after she recovered her breath.

"Nobody home yet," he said. "But I've invaded the kitchen and made fudge for us."

Tom led the way into the den where a plate of fudge was perched on the coffee table. Rachel stared at Thomas' masterpiece. Her brother had placed a pecan in the center of each tiny square. Rachel thought, "Perfect fudge made by a perfect brother!"

Tom flopped down in his favorite chair. "So tell me all about your life as a turbulent teen."

Rachel bounced from her thoughts back to Tom.

"I'm studying more."

"Yeah? You getting to be a grind?" He laughed in disbelief.

"People can change, you know. I have this terrific history teacher, Mr. Whelan.

He's helped me a lot."

"Whelan? Yeah, I heard about him. All the kids are supposed to be terrified of him. I was assigned a book he wrote when I was in college."

"You were?" Rachel hadn't even known he'd written a book! But it didn't surprise her. Mr. Whelan could do just about anything he wanted to, she thought. She made up her mind to get a copy and have him autograph it.

"Do you still have the book, Tom?"

"Yeah, I guess it's somewhere in my room. Probably in the closet with my other college junk."

"May I look for it sometime?"

"Sure, munchkin, help yourself."

"Why do you always call me 'munchkin'?"

"I've *always* called you that. You remind me of those weird little elves in the *Wizard of Oz.* You're so little and—"

"Funny looking," Rachel finished his sentence.

Thomas looked a little embarrassed. "Naw. Cute. I meant to say cute."

"I bet you don't date cute girls, huh, Thomas? You date pretty girls with long legs and hair down to their shoetops!"

Rachel recalled the beautiful girls Thomas used to date when he was in high school. She also remembered what he used to say about the "poor little bow-wows that nobody dated."

"I like all different kinds of girls," Tom said.

"Tom, do you think I'd look better if I cut my hair?"

"*What?* Cut your nice long hair? You've been growing it all your life. It'd be awful to cut it. You wouldn't be you anymore."

"I don't want to be me anymore. Not the me I used to be. I want to look prettier."

"Are you in love, munchkin?" Rachel's brother chuckled.

Rachel didn't answer him because she didn't know. She had so many strange, new feelings bubbling up inside that half the time she didn't even recognize herself.

Rachel used to dread looking at that

same sad, dull person in the mirror each morning. But now as Rachel looked in that mirror, she felt a smile forming. She was actually beginning to like what she found there.

That night, Rachel started her story for English. It was about the girl Rachel used to be:

> *Sometimes she wished she lived alone on a deserted island. But then, someone would call out her name, surprising her, forcing her to see she was not alone at all. She found this very painful because though she'd been surrounded by people all the time, so few had ever bothered with her. She would rather have believed she was alone. That would have justified how lonely she felt. It would have been all right to feel alone, if, indeed, she really were alone ...*

7

WHEN DENISE GOT home, Rachel cornered her. "Would I look good with short hair?"

Denise was grumbling about insensitive old Mark again. But she stopped long enough to look at Rachel.

She pushed Rachel's hair this way and that. Then she said, "I guess you would look better."

"Oh, Denny! I want to have it cut and styled."

"I'm going to Simone's on Saturday to get mine done. Why don't you come along with me, Rae?"

"That'd be great. I want it short and sort of like wispy curls in front."

"You know," Denise cocked her head and studied Rachel again, "you'd look much better that way. Funny, I never thought about it before. That long mop you've been carrying around doesn't do a thing for you."

At dinner that night, after Thomas told all about his financial successes, Rachel's mother turned to her.

"Rachel, I saw Carla Loring today and

she had some very good things to say about you."

"I'm starting to like school better. And I'm working harder," Rachel said, concentrating on her spinach. Rachel wasn't used to teachers saying good things about her. It was embarrassing, yet it was nice, too.

Rachel watched her father butter a biscuit. He really was a very handsome man with a great sense of humor and a big smile. That's why they picked him to anchor the local news.

Now he caught Rachel's eye and winked. "I hope your new interest in school isn't all because of that devilishly good-looking rogue of a history teacher."

Everybody chuckled and Rachel felt like two cents. She dropped her eyes and stared at her plate. She felt angry at her dad for doing it again. He always made her feel small and silly and stupid. He never did that to Denise. Or maybe he tried and Denise was just so sure of herself that she'd shoot back some wisecrack and get him to stop teasing her.

Denise had a great relationship with her dad. They were more like pals than father and daughter. But Rachel had this nagging feeling that she was a disappointment to her bright, handsome father. So when he teased her, it wasn't funny. It hurt.

Rachel took a deep breath and tried to explain. "Mr. Whelan has helped me a lot. I guess it's because he doesn't think I'm a clod. He's got me believing I'm *not* a clod, so I don't act like one all the time."

"Whoever said you were a clod?" Rachel's father asked. His eyes searched Rachel's. She felt like a poor butterfly stuck on a pin with huge eyes peering at her through a microscope.

"Nobody ever said so, Dad, but that's how I felt most of the time."

"Is he such a good teacher that he's inspired you to great heights of learning?" Rachel's father continued.

Rachel fell silent. She wished he'd just leave her alone and talk to Denise or somebody.

Rachel's mother filled in the gap.

"Carla says he's a terrible teacher. He's cynical and openly hates his students. He's snooty in the faculty lounge, too. He doesn't socialize with anybody. He even growls like an old bear when somebody suggests he might chaperone a dance."

"That's because he's so brilliant. He hates silly, trivial stuff," Rachel said, rushing to his defense.

"He wrote one of my college textbooks," Thomas commented.

"Really?" Rachel's mother gasped. "He hardly looks thirty years old and already he's authored a college text? He must have been a boy genius."

Rachel decided to change the subject. "I'm getting my hair cut Saturday."

"Why, you've had that beautiful long hair since you were a little girl!" Rachel's father clearly opposed her decision.

"I know, Dad, but I'm sixteen now. I want a change; I just want to look different."

Rachel followed this news quickly with her new social success. "Larry asked me to the junior picnic."

"All right!" Thomas approved. "He's one of the top jocks at Whitman."

On Friday afternoon, Thomas left. That was Rachel's chance to hunt for Mr. Whelan's book. She dug through three cartons of junk, old books, and tests before she saw the familiar name on the spine of the textbook: Whelan. The title of the book was *The Phoenician Piece of the Puzzle.* Rachel tucked the book under her arm and hurried to her bedroom.

The first thing Rachel read was about the author, Jeremiah Whelan.

> *Jeremiah Whelan assisted in several excavations in North Africa and has contributed numerous articles to archeological journals.*

He was famous! And he had chosen Rachel to work with him! For a few seconds, Rachel contemplated that tremendous thought. Then she sighed and tenderly laid the book on her bed.

Rachel was scared at Simone's on Saturday. She wasn't quite sure she'd made the right decision. In fact, she winced when her name was called.

She told the beauty operator in a hushed voice, "I'd like it if you could cut my hair like Audrey Hepburn's."

The lady was about the age of Rachel's mother. She laughed and said, "How does a girl your age know about her?"

But the beautician didn't wait for an answer. She immediately began snipping and clipping.

When she finished, Rachel looked in the mirror and gasped. She was sure she had made a horrible mistake. Her eyes looked huge. She was afraid she looked more like an alien than Audrey Hepburn. For years, Rachel had peered out from curtains of hair. Now those curtains were gone. Her plain face was naked, for all the world to see!

Rachel couldn't change what had happened, so she thanked the beauty operator and waited until her beautiful sister was finished.

All too soon Denise rounded the corner. When she caught sight of her little sister, she exclaimed, "Rae!"

"Oh! Please, *please* don't say anything! I know it's awful, but don't say it!" Rachel pleaded.

"It's terrific!" Denise said, laughing.

Rachel didn't believe her—or the rest of her family. Not until Sunday did her opinion begin to change. It was that afternoon, while she was sprinkling the lawn, that Larry came over.

The first thing he did was stop and stare. "You changed your hair," he said at last.

"Yeah. I had it cut Saturday."

"Looks great."

"Thanks." Rachel turned the nozzle to a fine spray and watched a rainbow form.

"You think you can go to the picnic with me?"

"I guess so." Rachel smiled at him.

"Super!" Larry was genuinely relieved. The he added with real warmth, "Hey, your hair really does look great."

He turned and ran back to his own

yard, grabbing a basketball by his garage door. He sank the first three baskets he shot. Rachel could hardly wait for school on Monday. She wondered what Mr. Whelan would think of her getting her hair cut just like he had suggested. Rachel figured he'd be happy that she had respected his opinion so much.

In history class, Rachel sat nervously awaiting his arrival. Maybe Mr. Whelan would see her and do a double-take. Maybe he would smile. Or maybe he would despise it.

Mr. Whelan came in briskly as usual. His fiery gaze swept over the class, including Rachel. There was no sign he noticed anything different about Rachel.

After class, Rachel went up to his desk with the book. Mr. Whelan was already madly stuffing his briefcase with papers.

"We'll be on our way in a minute," he said. "Got to take these infernal tests home and go over them. They're from second period. They're all idiots in second period. They're so awful, I can't even read the writing. Blast the stupidity of it all.

Why didn't somebody teach them pen-manship years ago before it was too late!"

Mr. Whelan was so angry, he broke the pencil he was stuffing into the case.

Rachel put the book on his desk. "I found this book you wrote, Mr. Whelan. I read it this weekend. It was really very interesting."

That wasn't true, of course. It was a dreadfully boring book, and Rachel couldn't imagine such an exciting teacher writing such a dull book. But still it meant a lot to her because he had written it.

"What?" he looked up sharply.

"This book," Rachel said, shoving it closer to him. "It was my brother's textbook in college."

He looked at the book as if it were a snake or something. Finally he said, "Oh, that thing. I'd forgotten all about it. It wasn't really a text. Some teachers just used it for additional reading. I didn't think there were any left. Actually, I'd hoped they were all shredded or burned."

"Oh. I thought it was a nice book," Rachel said, her mouth turning dry. "I thought you might autograph it for me."

"Autograph it?" He looked very strange, a little wild even, like he hated the book. Rachel couldn't understand this. She thought somebody would love a book they had written, no matter what.

"If it's not too much trouble. I mean, if you'd just sign your name . . . " Rachel's voice squeaked.

"Oh, no. Of course not." He scribbled his name on the inside cover and handed the book to Rachel. "Don't show this around. It isn't very good work."

"I won't. I just wanted it . . . for myself."

He quickly stuffed the last of his papers into his briefcase. A few tests escaped his grasp and fluttered to the floor. Rachel stooped for them at the same moment he did, and they almost bumped heads. Rachel hurriedly handed the tests back.

"Say," he said, "you did it."

"Did what?"

"Cut your hair. Looks excellent." He snapped his briefcase shut, and they headed outside.

"It must have been exciting to explore North Africa," Rachel said as they drove to the dig.

"What? Oh, yes. That was in the book, wasn't it? Well, actually, North Africa was too hot for me. I hate the heat. That's why I want to live at Monterey where it's cool."

"I guess most archeological digs are in hot places, huh? Even around here. It gets awfully hot in the summer."

Mr. Whelan cursed loudly as he pulled the camper up to the dig site. Rachel looked up. Two boys from Whitman stood over the holes in the earth. Rachel recognized them as Joe Chandler and Lee Rowan, big troublemakers who were always doing rotten things. They had sworn at teachers and even vandalized the school a couple of times.

Rachel was terrified, though not of the boys. It was Mr. Whelan's angry reaction that frightened her.

They screeched to a stop and Mr. Whelan leaped out. "You there! Damn it! What the devil are you doing here?"

"Wondering what all the digging is about, Teach." Joe put on an insolent grin.

"Yeah, you looking for gold?" Lee asked, his thumbs hooked into his belt.

"Look, you guys. It's just an old archeological dig," Rachel quickly explained. "You're not supposed to be stomping around here, so please just go away."

"Yeah?" Joe laughed. "I say it's public land and we got as much right as anybody else to be here."

Rachel hadn't really expected Joe and Lee would listen to her. They were the kind of guys who didn't respect anybody. Not teachers, not parents, not even the law. Rachel figured they hadn't been sent to juvenile hall only because their parents were big shots in town who pulled strings.

Abruptly Mr. Whelan turned and headed for the back door of his camper. Rachel could only think of one thing—

the gun! He was going to get the gun and something terrible would happen.

Rachel knew it was awful of her, but just now she didn't care if something happened to the two boys. What made her crazy with worry was the possibility that Mr. Whelan could get into deep trouble.

Rachel stepped forward. "You guys better beat it!"

She suddenly remembered something interesting she'd read in that big book. It was a chapter about curses at archeological dig sites. For example, some of the people who'd looked into King Tut's tomb died mysteriously. Some had been plagued all their lives by strange diseases and awful accidents.

Rachel began talking very fast. "The village that used to be here . . . they all died of a horrible sickness. It was called clovitis, and it was ten times worse than measles. The people got big splotches on their faces and all over their bodies and they died.

"Those clovitis germs could still be in

the dust. Mr. Whelan and I had to take shots so we wouldn't get it. But you guys—well, you better beat it fast."

The two boys stared at Rachel, wide-eyed and believing. Then within two seconds, they were hopping on Joe's motorbike and riding away as if the devil were after them. Lee hung on for all he was worth. He was clearly afraid he'd fall off in the dust and get history's worst case of clovitis.

Mr. Whelan stood at the back door of the camper. "Rachel, that was magnificent. How did you ever come up with that idea?"

"Oh, I know those big idiots. They believe anything. When I was in second grade, they were always stealing my chocolate chip cookies. They didn't stop until I told them my mother put bugs in our cookies to add extra protein. I said that the chocolate chips were actually chocolate-covered beetles."

Mr. Whelan's tenseness vanished in a hearty laugh.

Rachel and Mr. Whelan proceeded to

check the site. Everything seemed fine. "I don't think they were here long enough to mess anything up," Rachel said.

"Yeah, and I'll wager they won't be back, thanks to you, Rachel. You're really quick-witted."

Rachel laughed inside. Mr. Whelan believed she was smart while her own mother believed she was even too dumb to learn how to drive.

It was growing dark when the hour ended and Mr. Whelan said, "I'd better drive you home."

"No, it's okay. I can ride my bike."

He shook his head. "It'll just take me a few minutes. Perhaps we might even stop for something to eat. I feel hungry."

Rachel was overjoyed at the prospect. She and Mr. Whelan eating out together! It was almost a social thing, like colleagues would do.

They pulled into a drive-in. It turned out Mr. Whelan liked sweet and sour chicken and chocolate shakes as much as Rachel did.

As they sat there, he said, "You know,

I really lost my head when I saw those boys at the site. I might have done something I'd have regretted later."

He reached over and briefly covered Rachel's hand with his own. "Thanks for helping out so beautifully."

Rachel's whole body tingled. She thought if there really were such a thing as clovitis, she wouldn't mind having it if that were the price of this moment.

8 AS RACHEL STEPPED through the front door, Denise bounded down the stairs.

"So, now Mr. Wonderful is driving you home, eh?" Denise teased.

"He didn't want me biking in the dark," Rachel snapped. "He's very nice."

"I hope you're not falling in love with him, Rachel." Denise was serious.

Rachel was furious at her sister for spoiling her lovely mood.

"Are you crazy?" Rachel screamed. "You really do think I'm dumb, don't you?"

"Okay, okay. It's just that I flipped for my geology teacher at college. It hurt when I finally realized he was twice my age and considered me an immature twit."

Rachel's blood was boiling. She calmed herself enough to say, "Well, Mr. Whelan respects me like a real colleague."

The next day the teachers at Whitman had a workshop, so there was no school for the students. Rachel decided to go with Denise to her college campus, about eight miles from town.

"You'll probably be coming here, eventually," Denise said, "so you might as well look around."

Rachel enjoyed the drive through the olive green hills until the topic of conversation again turned to Mr. Whelan.

"I asked my anthropology teacher if there were any Indian artifacts around here. He said it was unlikely anybody would find anything of value," Denise said.

"Well, I've seen the pottery and the arrowheads with my own eyes," Rachel said.

"Maybe Mr. Whelan planted them," Denise said with a dumb giggle.

"That's the stupidest thing I've ever heard."

Denise shrugged. "I was only joking, Rae. But it does seem funny that all of a sudden a stranger comes in and finds a marvelous archeological site."

"He's a genius," Rachel declared firmly.

While Denise was in class, Rachel

prowled the library looking for Mr. Whelan's articles. She found one on an archeological dig in Israel and another one about North Africa. The articles, like the book, were dry and dull.

Rachel thought that was strange. Mr. Whelan was so sharp and funny in class. But maybe his articles had to be dry and uninteresting or the experts wouldn't take him seriously.

When Rachel and Denise got home, the phone was ringing. The girls' parents were both still at work.

Rachel grabbed the phone. When she heard the voice on the other end, her legs went numb. The voice belonged to Mr. Sherman, the principal. She had never in her whole life exchanged a word with Mr. Sherman. He only talked to the bright, active kids who were involved in student government—or the really rotten kids who were always in trouble.

Since Rachel fit into neither group, Mr. Sherman usually just ignored her. But sometimes Rachel would catch Mr. Sherman staring at her with a puzzled look, like he'd never seen her before and wondered if she were a Whitman student.

Yet now he was phoning the house when he knew her parents were still at work. Rachel had the sinking feeling that the call had to be about her.

"Yes, Mr. Sherman," Rachel said, wondering what misdeed she'd committed.

"I'm calling about the story you turned in to Ms. Loring for English," he said. He sounded very serious.

A cold sweat ran in rivers down Rachel's body. She'd been pretty honest in the story, describing many of her deep feelings. Maybe that had offended Ms. Loring and she'd complained to Mr. Sherman. That didn't seem possible, and yet . . .

"It was for an English thing," Rachel babbled foolishly. "I mean, Ms. Loring assigned everybody to—"

"Yes, I know. It's so good we want to put it in the annual literary magazine, *The Whitman Review.*"

Rachel's head began to spin. She'd seen

the fancy little book the English department put out every year. Most of the kids who had stuff in there were seniors who wrote poetry and angry articles about nuclear destruction or the environment. They were always the smart kids. The kind of smart kids you don't dare talk to if you're only a miserable sophomore or junior.

"You m-mean it, Mr. Sherman?"

"Why, yes, Rachel." He sounded like he was smiling.

"Oh, Mr. Sherman, that's so nice. That's wonderful!"

"Well, we're very proud of you here at Whitman. You'll be the first junior to have something in the *Review* in four years."

That evening, the whole Dorr family went to a restaurant to celebrate. It was kind of a tradition in the family that when somebody had a triumph, there was a special night out to celebrate. Rachel had gone to many celebrations for her parents and her brother and sister. This would be the first one for her.

"What's your story about?" Denise asked. "I tried to get a couple of my stories in *The Whitman Review,* but they didn't publish them. Yours must be really good, Rae. Everybody says the *Review* is the best high school magazine in the state."

"Oh, it's just this story I wrote about loneliness," Rachel said. "It's about a girl who felt like a nobody."

"My," Rachel's mother said, "imagine, a happy little thing like you writing a deep story about loneliness!"

Rachel smiled and said nothing.

"So we have a budding novelist in our midst," Rachel's father commented. "Who knows, Stella," he turned to his wife, "this little girl may end up surprising us all."

Rachel felt giddy as she ate the shrimp crepes and watched the flickering candles on the table. In a way, she was like Cinderella at the ball. And she couldn't wait to tell her prince what had happened.

After school on Monday, Rachel rushed to Mr. Whelan's desk and told him about the story. "It's just about the most exciting thing that's ever happened to me!"

He smiled and said, "That's marvelous!"

Rachel wanted to say more. She wanted to tell him that she owed her triumph to him because he'd believed in her and helped her believe in herself.

But she couldn't bring the words out. She felt them too deeply. She knew once she started telling him everything in her heart, she'd probably cry and make a fool of herself. She'd appear silly and unworthy of his respect.

So she just said, "I wanted you to know, Mr. Whelan," and then hurried away.

It was not exactly part of her triumph, but she began to enjoy another change in her life: Larry had started to eat lunch regularly with her. It was nice for her to have someone to talk to. Nice, that is, until that Wednesday, when Patty arrived at their lunch spot. Larry had been going with Patty just before he got friendly with Rachel again.

"Everybody is talking about your story that's going to be in the school magazine, Rachel," Patty said. Rachel wasn't sure if Patty was congratulating her, but she didn't think so. Patty looked like she'd just taken a big bite out of a lemon.

"Oh?" Rachel replied.

"Yes, you're a regular wonder lately. All of a sudden you have a new hairdo, a brand new brain . . . new friends. You're like Sleeping Beauty awakened by Prince Charming. Tell me, Rachel, is Larry your Prince Charming?" Now Patty sounded really bitter.

"Try to be a little less obvious, Patty," Larry said. His voice shook with anger. "Just get lost, okay?"

At that Patty stalked off. Larry grimaced as he watched her disappear, then turned to Rachel and smiled. "Don't mind little kitten-claws. She's always been catty. She's just mad I'm not taking her to the junior picnic."

"Why did you guys break up?"

"Well, she's kind of possessive. Anyway, she's yesterday's news." Larry lay back on the grass, his hands behind his head, a pleased look on his face.

Rachel sat beside him, feeling very cold and sad. His words kept turning around and around in her mind—"yesterday's news."

Though Rachel had never liked Patty, just now she felt sorry for her. All too often at Whitman, a girl's prestige hung on whether she had a steady guy or not. When the school was so small, everybody knew who was a social success and who wasn't. With the picnic coming up, all the conversation would be about who was going with who, and who—shame of shames—was going alone and belonged to the "dog club."

Rachel knew all about that. She'd been in the dog club so long, she'd almost stopped thinking about how ugly the name was.

"Don't look so sad," Larry said, reaching over and touching Rachel. For a minute he looked like he might pull her closer and kiss her. Rachel had seen him do that with other girls. But he must have seen something in her eyes that stopped him. "Rachel, what's up?"

"I don't know, Larry," Rachel said. Then, though she still had five minutes before the bell rang, she got up and headed for her next class.

And every step of the way, that phrase kept repeating in her mind in all its coldness. "Yesterday's news, yesterday's news."

9 WHEN RACHEL WENT to her locker that afternoon, she was shocked to find the door standing wide open. She was sure she'd locked it before going to lunch.

Her shock deepened when she found many of her things missing. Her English assignment which was due in five minutes was gone! Rachel searched frantically through her notebook, thinking she had just misplaced it. But it wasn't there.

"Something wrong?" The question came from Phyllis, who stood watching in the hall. She was a close friend of Patty's. They belonged to the same little group. Now she had a strange, half-amused smile on her lips.

"Somebody got into my locker and took my things."

"You shouldn't have left it open, Rachel."

"I didn't. Whoever did it must have watched me turn the lock and got the combination that way. Then they opened it while I was eating lunch."

It suddenly hit Rachel that Phyllis' locker was right next to hers. It would have been easy for Phyllis to have noted Rachel's locker combination.

"Well," Phyllis said, picking at her chipping red nail polish, "I guess those are the breaks. Some girls get their boyfriends stolen, and some girls get their class assignments snitched. I guess it all evens up in the end, huh?"

Rachel looked Phyllis right in the eye. She was amazed that she had the courage to stand up to aggressive Phyllis. "I didn't steal anybody's boyfriend."

"Really?" Phyllis' red lips parted over her even white teeth in an ugly smile.

"Yeah, really."

"Well, when little Miss Nobody suddenly thinks she's cool and takes my best friend's guy, then she's got to expect a few nasty things to happen to her, okay?" With that, Phyllis turned and strode away.

Rachel decided her only resort was to get her lock changed and be extra careful from now on. But for the moment, there was nothing left to do but trudge off to English class.

Of course when she got there, Ms. Loring didn't believe Rachel's explanation about the missing homework.

"I have more respect for a student who honestly admits not doing work and doesn't try to invent a silly story," she snapped, marking Rachel down.

Rachel didn't really blame her. A whole year of being a goof-off couldn't be erased by a few weeks of good work. Rachel could see Ms. Loring was disappointed. She probably thought Rachel was slipping back into her old habits.

Her last class that day was gym. Ms. Freeman ended volleyball ten minutes early so all the girls could shower, get dressed, and be out of school on time.

Patty was Ms. Freeman's TA, in charge of seeing that the balls were locked up properly and everything was left in order at the end of the day. Sometimes, like today when Ms. Freeman had a coach's meeting, Patty even locked up the gym.

Usually Patty was very fair, so the girls didn't mind her authority. But when somebody crossed her, she could get nasty.

"Rachel," she said, "your turn to check the showers and see if there's any mess." Patty had a blank look on her face.

Rachel couldn't see anything malicious in her eyes. "I had my turn already this week."

"You heard me," Patty barked. "Want a bad mark for being uncooperative?"

Rachel figured there was no use arguing. She went to check the showers. Then she quickly showered and dressed, except for her shoes and socks. They were stacked on the gym lockers.

By the time Rachel went to get her stuff, the gym was empty except for Patty, Phyllis, and two of their friends. They linked arms in front of Rachel and blocked her from getting her shoes and socks. They grinned and began singing the Whitman fight song.

"Win! Win! Win for Whitman!"

Rachel tried to squeeze past them to

her locker, but they continued to block her. "Let me through! I'm late!"

They danced in front of her, arms locked, making a solid wall and chanting.

"Win, win, win, with a yell and a grin,
Win, win, win for Whitman. Yehhhh!"

"Don't you understand? I'm late!" Rachel yelled.

"Aw, poor baby," Patty crooned, "I bet Mr. Whelan is waiting for you right now, huh?"

"Yeah," Phyllis joined in, "teacher's pet is gonna have a fit if she's late for Mr. Whelan."

"I'll tell Ms. Freeman what you did," Rachel screamed at Patty.

"Whatdahyah think, she's a dirty little fink," the girls chanted. "Put her in the well for the pigs to drink!" They screamed with laughter. They knew Rachel wouldn't tell on them. Anybody who did that could just forget about surviving at Whitman.

Tears filled Rachel's eyes, though she

desperately fought them back. "Let me through, you guys!" she demanded.

Finally they separated, and Rachel ran to her locker and grabbed her shoes and socks. Her socks had been knotted so tightly together that Rachel doubted they'd ever come apart. And her shoelaces were threaded together in a hopeless tangle.

Rachel didn't care anymore. She just wanted out of there. She raced down the corridor barefoot. Screams of hysterical laughter followed her as she ran towards the parking lot.

The camper had gone.

"Awww," Patty catcalled from the sidelines. "Teacher's pet missed her ride."

Rachel sat down on the curb and stuffed her socks into her school bag. Then she took out a pocketknife, cut through her shoelaces, and put on her shoes. Finally she climbed on her bike and pedaled towards the dig site. As she flew down the road, the wind blew the tears from her cheeks.

When she got to the site, Mr. Whelan

was already digging.

"I'm sorry I'm late," Rachel numbly apologized.

"I thought you were tied up at school and couldn't make it," he said. "You can start on that pile to your left."

Rachel nodded and went to work.

But the mechanical task of sifting the dirt didn't take Rachel's mind off what had happened that day. Nobody had ever bothered her at Whitman before. Nobody had ever played dirty tricks on her or given her any trouble. She always thought they had liked her a little.

Now she began to understand. She simply had never gotten into anybody's way before. She'd been too dull to compete with the bright kids for the top academic honors. And she wasn't pretty or popular enough to threaten their school offices, or, more importantly, their guys.

Now Rachel realized the bitter truth. It wasn't that they had liked her, at all. It was only that she had never *existed* until now. Suddenly it was Rachel shining in English instead of Phyllis. And suddenly it was Rachel—not Patty—that popular Larry was taking to the junior picnic.

Little Rachel Dorr had been nobody's competition for anything. She wasn't worth harassing, nor was she worth befriending. But now they were aware of her—and were going after her like an intruder who had broken into their midst.

Rachel slowly moved the sifting screen back and forth. Her tears flowed freely. She wasn't sure she could take it—their meanness, their dirty looks. How could she survive this?

Suddenly a shadow fell on Rachel's pile of dirt and a familiar voice asked, "What's this? My number one assistant crying on her artifacts?"

"Oh, I'm sorry," Rachel whispered, embarrassed that he should find her crying like a little kid. "It's nothing."

Mr. Whelan dropped to one knee and eyed one white sock sticking out of Rachel's school bag. He pulled it out and looked at the knotted mess. "Aha. This is what made you late. The wicked witches of Whitman got after you."

"It's just that ... that ... I guess they're jealous 'cause things are better for me now. I'm doing better in school, and a popular guy asked me to the picnic and—"

Rachel couldn't believe she was telling Mr. Whelan all of this. He couldn't possibly care about it. But as he stooped beside her, a change came over him.

Mr. Whelan didn't look like his usual cocky self—nor even his happy, relaxed, archeological-digger self. He looked rather boyish and helpless.

"You know those ninety-pound weaklings they used to describe in magazine ads for body-building equipment? These little wimpy guys on the beach with some big thug kicking sand in their faces? Maybe you're too young to have ever seen those ads. Anyway, when I was your age, I was one of those ninety-pound weaklings.

"I was at a boarding school. It was a rotten place. The stronger boys used to take out their loneliness and resentments on the weaker boys. It got so bad that I'd never have a blanket on a cold night: mine would be soaking wet in the bathtub. Or my entire wardrobe would be hung out on the flagpole on a cozy winter day.

"It was hell. All the little preppies who led charmed lives got their jollies by kicking me in the—" he frowned and turned away.

Rachel stared at him. "What did you do?"

"I got back at them on graduation day. I put one of them in a cast and another in the hospital. I hurt him badly. I imagine he still bears the scar.

"You see, what I lacked in physical strength, I made up for with hatred. I let them get to me. And that was stupid. I learned too late that I was a good, even a talented kid. I didn't have to prove that to anybody but myself. But by the time I learned that . . . well, I wasn't such a good kid anymore."

He continued, "Don't make that mistake, Rachel. Be strong and be proud.

You're special. Nobody can ever take that away from you."

Rachel was deeply moved he had taken the time to talk to her, to bare his own soul like this. In class, you would think he didn't care for the kids at all. But he did care. Rachel's heart filled with this realization.

She wanted to tell Mr. Whelan how much he meant to her, but again she stopped herself. Rachel was scared of setting something in motion that would soon be out of control. So she just smiled and hoped he could tell from her eyes how much she loved him.

10 IT WAS "JUDGMENT Day" in history class. But when Mr. Whelan returned the history tests, the judgment was wonderful. Rachel got a B.

Before this, she'd always gotten D's in history. But Rachel knew this was no gift. She'd earned every point.

Rachel quietly celebrated her good grade with Larry, and Patty happened to overhear. Patty's resentment was all too clear. Obviously she hadn't done as well on the test.

But Patty's bitterness didn't hurt so much anymore. Mr. Whelan's words helped soothe Rachel's pain. " 'Be strong and be proud,' " he had told her. She recited those words over and over. They were precious to her, just as he was.

At the dig that afternoon, old Mr. Leary came jogging by with his dogs. In the past, he hadn't stopped, but today for some reason he did.

"What are you digging for?" he shouted.

"Indian artifacts," Mr. Whelan replied.

Mr. Leary had lived in this area longer than anybody else. He was the unofficial town historian. Now he snorted at Mr. Whelan's claim.

"Huh! Nothin' like that in these parts. Only thing worth digging for around here is the Klepper gold." He chuckled to himself. "And people have been searching for that without much luck for nearly a hundred years."

The old story came back to Rachel. The first time she'd heard it, she was eight. Her grandfather had chosen a stormy night to tell her the tale of buried treasure.

It seemed that around the turn of the century, bank robbers had buried their loot near some white oak trees on the hill. No one knew which trees. Many had searched for the money, but no one had found anything. Naturally, the buried treasure became somewhat of a legend.

Mr. Whelan stared calmly as the old man continued.

"The Klepper boys supposedly buried the money somewhere along the foot of these hills. Said they marked the trees nearby with a V sign. Bunch of nonsense, if you ask me. Plenty of fools have wasted their time digging.'' He shook his head and then jogged away with his dogs.

"Well, he's a quaint fellow,'' Mr. Whelan said.

Rachel glanced up the hill at the row of eucalyptus trees. She saw something she had never noticed before. Hidden among the trees were the sawed-off stumps of some old gnarled white oaks.

"Something troubling you, Rachel?'' he asked, softly.

"No,'' Rachel said.

But all afternoon she thought about what Mr. Leary had said. Mr. Whelan seemed to suspect something, too. Every now and then he stared at her as though he realized she'd begun to figure out a terrible secret.

Most of the afternoon, Mr. Whelan did not dig. He'd never paused in his work before, but now he spent some time writing. Rachel told herself he must be correcting tests or writing an article for a magazine. But somehow, deep in her heart, Rachel didn't think he was doing either one.

At this time of year, the days were growing shorter and shorter. And now, so soon after they had begun digging, a silvery moon rose in the dusky sky. The mountains had grown dark and ominous—just like Mr. Whelan. A stranger wouldn't have noticed the change in his mood, but Rachel and her teacher were soul mates by now. She knew him well.

Rachel felt a chill touch her skin, then seep into her blood and bones. She thought this is how someone might feel who had just seen the beginning of the end of the world.

Once or twice Rachel glanced at the strikingly handsome man with the quicksilver eyes and rugged features. Again she thought how beautiful he was, not only on the outside—but more importantly—in his heart and soul.

They rode home together in silence. It was a dreadful silence, for unshed tears ached behind Rachel's eyes.

At last they reached Rachel's house and Mr. Whelan parked. Then he did something he'd never done before. He leaned over and kissed Rachel's cheek.

Then he pressed a sealed letter into her hand. For a brief moment, they looked at each other before Rachel got out of the camper. Neither one of them said a word.

It came as no surprise when Mr. Whelan did not come to school the next day. No surprise to Rachel, anyway. Old Mr. Leary had mentioned the digging to the sheriff, as both Mr. Whelan and Rachel knew he would. Questions were asked and an investigation was launched. It all came undone very quickly after that.

Mr. Whelan wasn't Mr. Whelan at all. He was David Sloan, an ex-convict from Buffalo. Mr. Sloan had educated himself in prison, where he had earned a Master's degree in history. It was in prison that he had learned of the Klepper gold.

When Sloan had been released from

prison, he'd taken on the identity of an unknown archeologist who had died in North Africa several years ago. The new Mr. Whelan used forged papers and got the teaching job to cover his digging. He was a smart man, they said, to have fooled everybody like that.

And now he had disappeared without a trace. He had left nothing but the mounds of dirt at the site. Nobody even knew if he had found the gold, but the sheriff thought he probably had.

"You shouldn't feel bad, darling," Rachel's mother said. "You didn't know what he really was. He used you, just like he used Whitman school. You were simply another one of his innocent victims."

Rachel pulled away from her mother. "I wasn't his victim."

She went to her room and locked the door. There she sat in the rocker and read Mr. Whelan's letter again. She had read it so many times, she'd almost memorized it.

Dear Rachel,

Because you're a bright girl, you know everything by now. What I am and what I've done isn't as important as something else I must say to you.

I've seen you grow and bloom, and I'm afraid you might believe you owe all of that to me. But I want you to see I didn't give you the brains to make that B in history. You had the potential all along. I didn't write that great story for the school magazine. You wrote it, Rachel.

And I didn't find the most valuable treasure on that hill. You did. People rarely think to look inside for buried treasure. Fulfill your great promise, Rachel.

> *Love,*
> *Mr. Whelan.*

After a month or two, Rachel read the

letter less often. His words were recorded
in her heart. And she no longer cared
what anybody said about Mr. Whelan. He
would always be the one who had shown
her just how many possibilities her life
held.

Rachel was finally able to put her
doubts to rest on her last visit to the dig
site. She marched straight up the hill to
the old oak trees and examined the dead
stumps.

Rachel did not expect to see the deep
holes inside each stump. They had obviously been made by some furry visitors
many years ago. The treasure hadn't been
buried at all. It had been in the trees all
the time. Mr. Whelan must have sawed
the tops completely off the stumps to
uncover the hiding place.

Rachel wondered when he had found
the treasure. Probably close to the day
when she spotted the chain saw. And yet
he had kept coming to the site after that.
Just to dig with her?

People rarely think to look inside for buried treasure.

Rachel sat down and leaned against the stump. She looked happily out over her hometown. Her family was starting to go out for celebration dinners for no reason at all. Larry was back with Patty, at Rachel's suggestion. And now Rachel was seeing a lot of Mark Pauling, a sweet guy who liked biology—and poetry. She was getting better grades in school, too. And everyday, she felt more and more like a Somebody.

Rachel smiled, thinking how good life was beginning to feel. She knew now that sometimes the best treasure *is* the one buried inside.

PASSAGES novels
by Anne Schraff

AN ALIEN SPRING
DON'T BLAME THE CHILDREN
THE GHOST BOY
THE HAUNTING OF HAWTHORNE
MAITLAND'S KID
PLEASE DON'T ASK ME TO LOVE YO
A SONG TO SING
SPARROW'S TREASURE
THE VANDAL
WHEN A HERO DIES

The Perfection Form Company
Logan, Iowa 51546